Scotch McBride

That Dark and Dreary Night

John Pirillo

Copyright 2022

DEDICATED TO SEAN CONNERY, WHO NOT ONLY MADE A GREAT JAMES BOND, BUT WAS ALSO A GREAT ACTOR.

WITHOUT HIS INFLUENCE I MIGHT NEVER HAVE MADE THIS SERIES OF BOOKS.

HIS SOFT SCOTISH BROGUE WILL NEVER BE FORGOTTEN, OR HIM!

A Pattern of Grace and Midnight Lace

Twixt sorrow and hate

Is a twisted narrow gate

Dark metal made of scorn.

And each day it stands

Between woman or man

Is a time to mourn.

In shallow depths

In hollow shades

Their plans made

Of ribbons and bows

Knives and guns

Sad and forlorn.

But neither he nor she

Shall see or find

Hope of release or relief

To save them from their fate this morn.

--Little John Cock Robin

A Flower here, a Flower there

Ms. May Mary Traymore eyed her backyard sternly, as if it offended her in some, deep unspoken way, then she brightened, and her wrinkled face softened. Wrinkles vanished in a flowering blossom of a smile. She went straight to a planter box with bright daisies about to pop their heads into the morning sunlight.

But instead of watering them, as she usually did this time each morning, she went to the fence separating her yard from the next.

In that yard an older man sat back on a reclining wooden chair in his yard, eyes shut.

May sent him a kind thought. Old Man Warren was near his death. He had no one. She always made it a point to do something, she hoped, that brightened his day, offered a light of hope to what he assumed was an ending darkness.

He was not a negative man, but he was facing that part of life that all must...eventually.

She looked away from him, then went to another planter box where bright sunny, marigolds were proudly standing up, showing off their golden faces. She took the shearing knife from her apron pocket and approached the largest marigold. "Please don't mind if I cut you, it's for worthy cause."

She listened several moments as if hearing an answer from the flower, then cut the marigold free of its stem.

She held it up with a smile. "You will do quite nicely.

May went to the gate that opened between her home and Old Man Warren's and cautiously opened it so not a sound was made, then tiptoed across the intervening grass and laid the Marigold in her right hand gently across his lap.

Old Man Warren wiggled his nose once, as if sniffing the flower, but did not waken. She gave his forehead a kiss, then tiptoed back to her own yard and shut the gate. Again, as quietly as she opened it.

"There," she said happily.

She then went to her back porch and picked up a small sack of breadcrumbs she saved from the week before. She went to the base of a nicely carved fountain with a bowl at its top that was dry. She spread the breadcrumbs inside, then walked away.

A fluttering of wings announced the little friends of the air who had been watching and waiting for her. She walked back to her porch and sat down to view and enjoy

all the birds now filling the bowl and having a meal.

She smiled.

Her eyes began to flutter, as if weighted down, then she yawned.

Mother Spoon's Tea Shop

Mother Spoon, also known as Kate Barnett Brian, topped off Scotch McBride's teacup then Detective Margaret Mallory's.

"You're too kind," Scotch told her.

"And if I am not, where would me thanks be?"

Margaret laughed. "I doubt anyone would dare leave your shop without tipping you."

Mother Spoon touched a silver spoon to her beak nose. "Better not, or I'll haunt them when I pass over."

Scotch laughed as Mother Spoon hobbled off, her right leg shorter than her left, and made of wood. Mother Spoon would do no such thing. People gave her tips even when they ate nothing because of her kindly nature, quick wit, and gentle ways.

"A good woman."

Margaret lifted her teacup. "And more importantly, she knows how to make the brews she serves strong enough to shake off a bad night."

"So, Margaret, how has your week been so far?"

Margaret patted her bun of hair. "Why? Does it show?"

Scotch laughed. He loved the fact that Margaret was not a frivolous woman, was smart, and had a profound sense of humor and self-deprecation. It also did not hurt any that she was remarkably attractive as well.

He reached a hand across the small polished white table to pat her right hand. "Never."

Margaret leaned forward and looked into his eyes. Their faces several inches from each other now. "You surely know how to shore up a woman's self-esteem."

"And you," Scotch replied, squeezing her hand warmly. "Know how to make a man feel sunshine in the midst of a chilly day."

Margaret leans closer, shutting her eyes.

Scotch is about to kiss her, when…

"Hurry, Inspector Dublin needs you two now!"

Scotch and Margaret pull back to look at who spoke. It was a constable, a worried look on his face. His large body sticking halfway in the door of the shop and halfway out. "He said hurry!"

Scotch sighed, let go of Margaret's hand. "He always says that."

He nodded to the constable. "Tell him we are on our way."

The constable exited.

Scotch rose. "Well then, I suppose me scrambled eggs are better than nothing for breakfast."

Margaret gave Scotch an inquiring look. "But Mother Spoon doesn't serve scrambled eggs."

Scotch laughed. "Neither does Inspector Dublin. It is best if we hurry."

Scotch left cash on the table, then exited holding the door open for Margaret, who followed him out.

Mother Spoon eyed the plate of untouched scones on the table and clucked like a hen. "I surely hate throwing away these."

She grinned when she felt a familiar presence behind her. "But perhaps, you know someone who might have a taste for them?"

"Cock surely would!"

She heard a rustling behind her and turned. Mother Spoon was grinning from ear to ear and holding out a bag she had filled with the scones. "Take them. A handsome young man like you should not go to work without a hearty meal."

Cock John Robin felt no shame in taking the scones.

"I finished cleaning up the kitchen, Mother Spoon."

She smiled. "I hope you ate something after you did."

He rubbed his stomach and rolled his eyes. "I most certainly did."

She leaned over and gave Cock a kiss on hir head. "Love you."

He grinned. Bowed. "And you are the sunshine of me heart too!

Mother Spoon wagged a finger at him. "Admit it, Otter, you love me's scones, not me."

"That too," he replied with a grin. Gave her a wink and left through the front door.

Mother Spoon sighed. "Always coming and going, but none ever staying."

She burst into a yawn, then a smile, began humming a tune and headed back to the kitchen where she was quite certain it was still a mess.

The Mystery Begins

May Mary Traymore woke up with a stiff neck. It was not the usual sort that felt like you neck was at the wrong angle and hurting.

It was worse.

She rubbed at her neck with her hand.

Then froze.

What?

She carefully traced the shape against her neck which had shocked her.

A hand.

With fingernails that were overly long.

She jerked her hand away in fear.

But nothing happened.

The hand did not move.

Her neck did not stop aching either.

She sat up abruptly and then in the pale light of the waning moon through her balcony window, saw what was now on her hand which had touched her neck.

She screamed.

The Harrowing

"Horrible. Simply disgusting."

Scotch shook his head but did not comment. He just waited while Little Cock John Robin polished his shoes. He had an important meeting with the Town Jaspar. A special position that needed a man look his best, even if the man's peculiar station in the small town of Eagerly was a joke at best. Still, he had to give the man his due.

Town Jaspar Mark Stimson claims he is descended from leprechauns, which surely were more important on the Island of Ireland, than in the land of Scotland. But one cannot argue with fate or with destiny...especially when both were wrapped up in an old man who was both a priest and a well-respected man.

Even if the town was merely a small dot on the map of Scotland.

Little Cock John Robin finished the work he had begun, shoved his stool back and admired the glow of his whiskery chin on the face of Scotch's shoes.

"Mind if I don't."

"Don't what, Cock?"

Little Cock John Robin gave Scotch a wide lipped grin, causing his caterpillar mustache of bright red hair to squirm like a trapped insect in a bottle. He leaned closer and cupped a hand to his mouth and whispered, "Tell ye the truth, man."

"Which is?"

Little Cock John Robin glanced about to make sure no one was near and then said, "The Harrowing."

With those two words, he grabbed his box of shoe polish, brushes and clothes and walked briskly away, whistling a Scottish tune about ghosts and fidgets that bounce in the night.

Scrambled Eggs

"You like scrambled eggs, Mister McBride?"

Scotch uncrossed his right leg from over his left and leaned forward from the antique chair with golden, wood arms that he sat upon and eyed Madame Crystal thoughtfully. "Why do I get the feeling this is not going to be about breakfast?"

She smiled. "When one is in the mood to feed the soul, then it is important to start with a healthy meal."

Scotch scratched his scruffy beard, then nodded. "Sounds reasonable, though a bit on the mystical side to me."

He gave Madame Crystal a cock-angled grin, then said, "But then of course, not much about you that isn't mystical."

Madame Crystal laughed so hard that the folds of fat on her neck jumped up in down like clapping hands. She stopped and leaned forward from her wide couch she sat upon. She pointed a finger at Scotch, wagging it several times as if scolding him.

"Flattery will get you nowhere, young man."

The large ruby ring on the finger she was pointing at him caught flashes of candlelight and reflected them into Scotch's eyes.

"Wisdom can come from anywhere, Mister McBride."

"But not usually for breakfast," Scotch pointed out.

Madame Crystal broke into laughter again and leaned back onto her couch. She pulled a thick woolen blanket over her legs and sighed. "Mortal man lives like a snail in its shell, only poking its head out of its shell when it feels safe."

"I don't understand," Scotch replied. This woman was always a surprise to him. Her remarks made his brain buzz like a honeybee about a huge nest of honey, but he liked the challenge of being with her. She was evanescent in a way he had never experienced with anyone else.

And she fed not only his brain, but his heart. She was the most loving woman he had ever met, even though to most men who just saw her from a distance and did not know her, might think she was just another obese woman.

"Of course, you do not, Detective McBride. You have not had your scrambled eggs yet," she said, but with an ounce of laughter following her words. But her eyes danced with amusement.

And something else he could not define.

It was if someone else were peering from behind her eyes, a second person of such power that it made him feel like a small child before their huge father.

But it was not frightening, so much as humbling, that look. Because there was not a grain of judgement in that look, only an incredible depth of compassion unlike any he had ever known before.

The Long Sleep

Inspector Dublin eyed the woman on her bed, and the large fish with the detached hand affixed to its head.

"A pity."

Scotch nodded. "The brutality of such murders escapes me. What reasonable purpose can such a bizarre death bring to a person's heart?"

Detective Margaret Mallory shuddered. "If they have one."

Scotch glanced at her, gave her a sympathetic look. "Everyone has a heart; just that some choose not to share it with others."

Inspector Dublin eyed the large fish laying on the woman's bed, with a detached hand affixed to its head. "Rather drastic way to amuse oneself."

Scotch looked at the woman's body that lay next the fish. Her eyes stared off into nothing. Her lips were blood-stained. Her right hand was missing. "I suspect no one laughed."

"No one sane!" Detective Margaret Mallory added.

Inspector Dublin nodded. "I agree. See here, McBride, what do you make of this note?"

Scotch nodded to the M.E. "You may remove Ms. Traymore now, but I want to know if you discover any extenuating evidence."

Sir Flim O'Brien, an older man nodded. His white hair seemed to rest uneasily on the shoulders of his white suit as he folded May Mary Traymore's arms over each other. He bowed his head in silent prayer, then nodded to his assistants, who respectfully removed her body to a stretcher to take out.

Sir Flim O'Brien followed them out of the bedroom.

Inspector Dublin turned to Scotch. "Can you see now why I was so urgent about getting the two of you here this morning?"

Detective Mallory answered for Scotch. "The Sunset Murders."

Inspector Dublin sighed. "Yes. But how can that be? We brought that killer to justice."

Scotch cocked an eyebrow on the Inspector. "Justice is like scrambled eggs, Inspector."

Detective Margaret Mallory gave him a surprised look. He grinned at her. "Lot of those this morning, evidently."

"Oh?"

"Because, Inspector, what often it starts out as scrambled eggs, soon turns into an omelet in disguise."

Inspector Dublin coughed into a hand. "In God's name, McBride, where in the world do you come up with such analogies?"

Otter and Scotch answered at the same time. "Madame Crystal."

Inspector Dublin shook his head and hurried after the M.E., muttering unhappily. "Why do I ever even ask?"

Detective Margaret Mallory grabs McBride's arm before he can leave. "I think I've found something interesting, Scotch?"

"Of what kind?"

The Garden of Fools and Tools

Little John Cock Robin looked up from a planter box he is watering with a small bucket. Its red handle glitters with the sweat of moisture, as does his forehead.

He cocks his head to wink at Scotch as he walks up with Detective Margaret Mallory. "Greetings."

"Cock, you're here!"

"As surely as the sweat on my brow and the horse in the meadow."

"We are in the city of Glasgow. There is no meadow here," Margaret pointed out with a frown. She turned to Scotch. "Now you see why I thought this might be of help?"

"I do not, Scotch replied with a slight grin. "Cock's a bit..."

"Touched?" Cock finished for Scotch. "Indeed I am. By angels and by God."

"Not what I meant!" Margaret scolded. "It what he told me earlier."

She turned to Cock. "Please, tell him what you told me."

Cock chuckled, then finished his watering and turned to them to give his full attention. "Don't you find it strange, Scotch, that a woman who was as kind as Mary was, and as sweet to all life as could be, should abandon her flowers?"

Margaret turned her back to Cock, "Scotch! This has to be important!"

Scotch winked at Cock, who took the hint and scrambled away, scampering about like a small child loose in a candy store. First checking a rose bush, then a daisy, then a piece of fence, then a cart, then a shovel and rake, until he finally exited through a white gate.

"Odd sort!" Margaret commented, grateful the man was gone.

"He means well."

"His might mean well, but..." She shivered. "He still gives me the midnight creeps."

"Midnight?" Scotch asks.

"Yes, the kind you get when you're at the height of an investigation and close to solving it, and then the criminal shows up with a gun or knife to kill you."

Scotch raises an eyebrow and searches the cloudy sky above. "Looks like it's going to be another dark and dreary night."

Margaret punctuates his observation with a new shiver.

Scotch's eyebrows scrunch together in thought.

"Exactly!" He lets out in an explosion of relief. "Now I know what Madame Crystal meant by scrambled eggs!"

"What does scrambled eggs have to do with anything but breakfast?" Margaret asks.

Scotch turns to Margaret. "I do not know. But I do know that I am going to take a wee trip to the local library."

"Why?" Margaret asks.

Library

Scotch steps through the revolving glass doors at the front of the library and heads at once to the Librarian at the front desk.

She looks up from a book she is reading. An annoyed look shoving her beak nose upwards beneath a pair of black rimmed bifocals that have seen better days.

"The Adventures of Sherlock Holmes," by Sir Arthur Conan Doyle." Scotch grins. "Great author."

She looks at Scotch with a frown. "It's really John Watson who wrote these stories, you know."

Scotch chuckles. "I've heard that said by some."

"What can I do for you, sir?" She asks, unmollified by Scotch's attempt at humor.

"I'm looking for scrambled eggs."

"Pardon me?"

"I mean books on them. Anything unusual especially."

"Will this be for business or pleasure?"

"Oh, most certainly business. Know this will more than likely take up much of your time, but if you can spare this lad a bit of your precious time, it would be much appreciated."

Scotch takes a card from his wallet and hands it over to her. "Official police business, I'm afraid."

"Where's your badge?"

Scotch leans closer, then whispers. "I am undercover. No one needs to know I am here."

She eyes the card again, then sighs. Nods. "Very well, after a dark and dreary night, I suppose a dark and dreary day is to be expected."

She rises from her chair and motions for Scotch to follow her.

Not one to waste words, or a smile, thought Scotch as he followed her. Well, not all librarians hand out lollipops.

He chuckled at his mental joke.

She looked back at him; her nose pushed even higher in annoyance. Her bifocals threatening to launch off her nose. "Kindly keep your voice down. This is a library."

"Sorry."

She sighs, then continues to bring them along a winding series of rooms that open into smaller rooms, connected by dustier and dustier floors. They pass through a labyrinth of bookcases that rise from floor to ceiling.

The librarian speaks again. "Some librarians in the past claim to have heard ghostly voices where we are going."

"Do you believe them?"

"It's not ghosts I worry myself over," she replies in an annoyed voice.

She finally stops before a door marked *Restricted*.

"I hope you don't mind a wee bit of dust, Mister McBride?"

"I do not." *As if they had not already raised enough dust to start a storm in the Sahara Desert.*

"Good, because this is a wee bit more than most are used to," the librarian replies, opening the door to reveal a staircase leading downwards.

Vault of Legends

Scotch's eyes widen as they stop at the bottom of the staircase before a huge bank vault like door. Motes of dust float about them like a swarm of gnats from the hugely dusty steps they just descended.

But oddly, the floor is free of dust.

Scotch frowns. There is something to this ghost thing after all. And when the librarian turns to look at him, she has a ghostly look to her, which adds to the sudden discomfort Scotch has been feeling.

"We try to keep our rarer books in a room that is better for preserving paper."

"A bank vault?"

"Don't you make fun of a bank vault, Detective McBride, it's also what keeps your cash safe from molding as well."

"I thought it was the chemicals they printed on the paper that did that job."

She frowned at his dismissal and without another word, reaches for the wheel handle of the door, spins it twice one way, then three times the opposite, then once the other and pulls.

The door opens, its ancient hinges complaining.

Ancient Books

"Few in Glasgow know of what we keep here, and you are the first in my entire career here in this library, who has asked for what we keep here."

"I am honored then."

"No, you're not," she said.

Reminding Scotch once more that this woman must have a very, very lonely love life. How anyone could have a life partner with the attitude of this woman was beyond him.

Scotch peered into the dry vault, where thousands of books filled old wooden shelves from the hard floor to the ceiling. Each book in alphabetical ordered.

"And what exactly is it you have for me here?"

The librarian peered into Scotch's face and grinned.

He almost laughed, because she obviously did not grin often, or her makeup would not be cracking like it was now. But he did not laugh.

She waved at the bookshelves. "Everything that has ever been written about the Druids is kept down here."

She peered at his face thoughtfully a moment.

"Few know that the Druids were more than just dark sorcerers. Cruel men who once dominated our world with brutality and acts of extreme violence."

"And what did we not know?" Scotch inquired politely.

The right response. The librarian's face lit up with satisfaction. Obviously, few gave her the opportunity to show off her historical knowledge.

He smiled. "Please. History is exactly what I am looking for."

The light in her face exploded into a bonfire.

She leaned closer to him and putting a hand to the side of her mouth, as if about to reveal dangerous, and very secret information. She whispered. "They collected history and recipes."

"Fascinating."

The librarian stepped to the left wall of books and gestured with a shaking hand the top shelf. "These are the books you seek."

She pointed to a stepstool near her. "You can use this to reach them."

She headed for the way out. "Just close the door once you are through. There is a door out from this floor to the left once you exit the vault, so you do not need to return upstairs if you do not wish."

"That's handy."

She gave him a smile that made his blood freeze.

"It had to be. The Druids carved the whole of this floor from solid rock, and sometime when it rained, it would flood. They had to have another way out in an emergency."

"Interesting.

She leaned closer; her eyes lit with mirth. "Also, it was used to drown their victims when they had to hurry off for dinner."

Scotch had no reply to that.

She laughed. "Have an interesting time, Detective McBride."

"I'm certain I will," he confided.

He turned to look at the shelf to which she had pointed. "There must be a hundred books on that shelf alone at the very least!"

He turned to see if she had any comment, but the librarian had already vanished.

"I wonder if the ghosts are afraid of her," he mused, then turned about to grab the stepstool to reach the books. He took the very first one down to examine it.

"When is a scrambled egg not a scrambled egg?" He read. He frowned. He examined the author's name a moment. *Professor Duck Mingallo.*

Then an alarming sound caught his attention. The huge vault door was swinging shut. Groaning loudly but closing swiftly.

He dropped from the stool and ran for the closing door, but he was too late.

He had to fall back from the crushing weight of the immense vault.

It shut with a hollow, smooshing sound, then the room went utterly dark.

Old Man Warren's

Detective Margaret Mallory knocked on the door of May Mary Traymore's neighbor, Mr. Warren. Margaret slipped her foot from her left shoe and rubbed her heel a moment. "Chafing, drat it all!"

She hurriedly put her shoe back on at the sound of approaching footsteps.

Undoubtedly the pain was from the pebble she had just freed from its nest in her shoe, but she would check it out further once she got back to her car.

The front door opened.

She smiled at the man who frowned up at her.

"What do you want?"

"I'm so sorry to bother you Mister Warren, but I'm here on official business." She tapped the badge displayed prominently on her blouse.

He glared at it. "I do not like the police. I hate police. They never catch the criminals and eat too many doughnuts!"

"Oh, we catch a few now and then. And doughnuts are quite tasty with a fresh cup of hot coffee."

His sour look turned into amusement. "You're a sassy sort, aren't you?"

"I've had a lot of practice," she confided with a warm smile.

He barked with laughter. "Where were you when I was single and young?"

"Sorry. Happens sometimes."

He laughed further. Then he stopped, gave her a suspicious look. "You are not here to arrest me for chasing the dog off my lawn, are you? A hundred lawns up and down the street, and they always choose mine to dump on. Such a bother."

He shook his head, then investigated her face again. "I do not appreciate the bother of cleaning up after them. And I also do not like police nosing into my business!" He said firmly.

"And believe me, Mister Warren, we don't like bothering you."

"Then why are you here?"

She gave him a surprised look. "You don't know?"

"Know what?"

"Oh dear. I hate to be the one to tell you, but your neighbor, Ms. May Mary Traymore is dead."

Mr. Warren reacted as if someone had slapped him in the face. "Dead!" He choked out. "No!"

He collapsed into Margaret's arms.

Library Vault

Scotch sighed in the dark of the vault. "If I were Sherlock Holmes, what would I do at a time like this?"

He laughed. "If I were Sherlock Holmes, Scotch McBride, we wouldn't be stuck in this silly predicament now, would we?"

The sound of a match striking.

"Good thing I keep these for the Inspector's pipe."

Scotch's face blazed to life. He held the match away from him and examined the huge vault door for any kind of emergency release.

"Ow!" He cried out and dropped the match.

He stomped it out on the floor.

Absolute darkness again.

"Truly this is turning into a difficult day," Scotch sighed. "And me forgetting to bring along me stress ball today."

He lit another match.

Book Vault

Scotch dropped his fourth and next to last match on the floor and stomped it out. "No way out. None!"

He sat down on the floor and shook his head in disgust. "What would Sherlock Holmes have done in my place?"

He sighed deeply and made himself as comfortable as possible on the floor. "Beating myself up for nothing, surely."

He chuckled. "Surely, the librarian will come looking for me."

Then cold logic struck like an arrow through his heart. The librarian would have no way of knowing he was still in the vault. And from what he had seen found anything besides reading her Holmes books annoying and a waste of time.

Weariness settled in suddenly, settling over him like a friendly, warm blanket.

He shut his eyes.

Did not make any difference it they were open or not in here. As dark with them open, as closed.

He felt sleep gently nudging at his senses, then as he struggled to resist the hug of sleep, a light came on at the back of his mind. An idea that just might work. If he could keep awake long enough to do it.

Then he began seeing himself back home with his father and Madame Crystal at the dinner table.

'Son, I hope you like your breakfast. Madame Crystal and I put it together for you. You need to keep your strength up son, you have been pushing yourself too hard."

Scotch chuckled. "Since when has any meal ever made that big of a difference?"

Then the kitchen door opened, and the librarian walked out with a bloody apron wrapped around her waist. She carried a silver tray with white daisies on its edges. Seated center of the tray was a golden baking pan, steam rising from it.

She set it on the table. Smiling, she said, 'Eat up before it chills."

In the baking pan was a giant fish with a severed hand attached to it.

Mr. Warren's Living Room

"Dead?" Mr. Warren shook his head. "Impossible!" But he knew she was not lying. He could tell by the look on Detective Mallory's face.

He dropped the wet towel she had applied to his forehead to help him awaken and sat up on the sofa she had lain him.

"Why do you say that?" Detective Margaret Mallory asked.

She grabbed the wet towel before it could soak into his sofa and laid it on the coffee table between them.

"Thank you," Mr. Warren said, his voice empty and shallow sounding. He looked up at her. "I don't deserve such treatment after the way I…"

"No bother. Please. Do finish what you were about to say."

"Because she kissed me on the forehead just this morning."

Detective Margaret Mallory shivered in alarm. That was impossible. Ms. Traymore was murdered the day before!

"Who kissed you?"

Mr. Warren sighed. "Right here." He poked his forehead. 'She always plants one here on me shiny forehead when I'm napping."

He snorts. "Always thinks I am still asleep. But I am not. He begins to shiver, then tears well up in his eyes. "Dead."

He puts his head in his hands and sobs.

Detective Margaret Mallory sits next to him and puts an arm about him. He slowly stops sobbing. "Please, Mister Warren. I know this is hard on you, but you need to be clear on this."

He shakes his head in assent but does not open his eyes. "I'm sure."

"You said she was here this morning."

"Yes. Where else could she have been." He rapped his knuckles against the metal of the walker that he was using to get around with.

Its hollow ring haunted the sudden silence between them. Shocked Mr. Warren enough for him to sit up. He glanced into Detective Margaret Mallory's eyes. Shook his head slowly. "Sorry. This has left me..." He began to weep again.

Detective Margery Mallory hurriedly handed him a Kleenex and he blew into it. Finished, he clutched it between his hands, which were pale as a ghost from squeezing together so tightly.

He gave her a weary, sad look. "I do not get around that much these days." He tapped his walker. "But when I do get…around…as you might think. It is only to my backyard and a lawn chair I have placed there for naps."

"Sorry."

Detective Margaret Mallory gave him a sympathetic look. "That must be hard on you."

He gave her a surprised look. "You are the first intelligent person who has not pretended I am not old and dying. I thank you for that."

Detective Margaret Mallory laughed. "You don't look that ready to drop into the grave."

His face sagged into a weary smile. "Believe me, when you get to the age where a beautiful woman like you is more important as someone to talk with than rattle the sheets of my bed with…"

Detective Margaret Mallory laughed again. "I am sorry to hear that. Or should I say, glad."

He sighed. Then gave her a second glance, this time examining her more closely. "Very well. I suppose it's nice to have company, even if only for the wrong reasons."

He winked at her. "And only for decoration."

Excuses, Excuses

Scotch gasped for air, suddenly shaken from darkness reaching out for him. He heard the vault opening and tried to break out of his hiding place. "Help!" He cried out.

The boxes about Scotch fell away as hands reached for him. At the same time, he could hear the hiss and spit of water and chemicals sloshing into the vault, and then him and the men rescuing him.

He was helped to his feet by strong hands, choking still, and gagging.

"Easy. You are safe now." A man's voice soothed him.

His gamble had paid off.

The fire alarm, ancient no doubt, still worked.

But he had not thought he would make it. He had made a small igloo of sorts to protect as much air as possible, and then lit the fire and climbed inside the igloo and when the smoke began to fill the air, shut its entrance.

And that is where they had found him when they opened the giant vault door.

He was barely conscious when he heard the boxes around him scattered, then strong hands and arms gathered him to lay him down on a stretcher. Give him oxygen.

The librarian hovered over him, a worried look on her face. "I am so sorry, Detective McBride, I had no idea you were trapped inside the vault. None whatsoever. I should never have left you alone in there."

Scotch took the oxygen mask off his face, then sat up on the stretcher and stood from it. He wobbled a moment unsteadily, but after more deep draws on the oxygen, he lifted its mask and replied.

"It is not your fault. It is an old vault. I am sure it was just age kicking in."

The librarian looked relieved and backed out of view.

The Chief Fireman smiled at Scotch. "This old vault should have shut years ago. He made a sour face. "Remember hiding in it as a child. Even then it was not a safe place to be."

Scotch gave him a surprised look. "Truly?"

"Aye, indeed. As a wee laddie I would sneak down here to eat chocolates me Auntie Faucet gave me when me Mum was not watching."

The Chief Fireman leaned closer. "You have met her. You can see why I did not want to be on the wrong side of her."

Scotch's eyebrows rose. "The librarian's your Mum?"

The Chief Fireman grinned. "Never want to get on the wrong side of that woman, even now. She has a temper like a hurricane exploding from a good bottle of Scotch, if'n your gits me meaning, Detective?"

Scotch smiled. "Fortunately, I haven't had that pleasure."

"How's your chest feeling?"

"Better now. Thank you, I will be fine now. I did not breathe too much of the smoke. I meditated, which reduced my need for oxygen."

The Fire Chief shook his head. "I meditate too, but even so, you're lucky this vault has the old alarm still working inside it, or you'd be crispy bacon when we finally found you."

Scotch cocked an eyebrow. "What do you mean?"

"You've been in that old beast of a vault for nearly two days now."

Scotch sat back down on the stretcher. "Maybe I will let you carry me out after all."

The sound of someone fighting to get through the crowd of firefighters, a woman's voice, then Detective Margaret Mallory plunges into view.

"Scotch!"

She rushes to him and gives him a hug. "Thank God you're alive!"

She began sobbing into his neck.

He gave her a reassuring hug. "As meself is as well, dear Margaret. As meself!"

She let go, and then, for the first time, saw the damage inside the vault. A good part of the bookshelf on the right side was a dark mound of charred paper and wood now.

Scotch snickered. "Fortunately, for history's sake, the only books damaged were the Druid recipes for mushroom and moss soup."

He chuckled. Then lost his smile "And scrambled eggs."

Margaret punched him lightly on the shoulder. "Sometimes, McBride your humor can be almost as bad as those recipes!"

He stood up from the stretcher and drew her to him. She began sobbing again.

The firemen all drifted away, as did the librarian, who glanced back once at the two hugging and then left up the stairs. The look on her face was not pleasant.

Only one person did see it, her son, the Chief Fireman. He nodded to his men, and they began cleaning up the mess in the vault.

The Forensics Team who had been taking pictures and samples for evidence of the fire gathered their equipment and went upstairs.

Scotch gently unentangled Detective Margaret Mallory from him and looked into her eyes. "I hope you had better luck than I these last few days."

He gave her a handkerchief from his jacket. She wiped her eyes, then blew her nose. She did not give it back. "Smells like smoke!"

"Sorry!" He smiled. She knew he would just throw it away.

She investigated his face. "I phoned Inspector Dublin before I rushed here. He has arranged for us to speak with the suspect tomorrow morning."

Scotch frowned. "Suspect?"

"Yes. I have one. Though he is not likely involved."

Scotch lowered his voice. He began leading her to the stairs. "Let us talk about your suspect...outside. I had this dream I just remembered."

He stopped to look at her. "Do not laugh. It was about scrambled eggs. Sort of."

Interrogation Room

"Why in God's name have you called my mother and I here, Detective McBride? I saved your life. She is just a librarian!" The Chief Fireman growled.

Scotch paced in front of a chalk board, hands behind his back.

Detective Margaret Mallory sat at the entrance to the room and Inspector Dublin sat to the left of her, arms folded, his face expressionless...which did not bode well for someone this morning.

Scotch paced a few moments longer, then turned to glance at Mr. Warren, the librarian, and the Chief Fire Man.

"It's not every day that a good woman like May Mary Traymore is found dead...of strangulation and mutilation, Chief."

'True. But still..."

Scotch waved the Chief off. The man glowered at Scotch but shut up.

Mr. Warren rattled his walker parked next his chair at the witness table. "I need me nap."

Scotch chuckled. "Do not worry, Mister Warren. We will have Detective Mallory here, drive you home after we are through here."

"If you are so sure I am going home afterwards, then why am I here at all? It makes no sense to me. I want to go home now. I need me nap in the sun."

Scotch ignored him, then turned to the librarian. "How long did you know, Ms. Traymore?"

The librarian gave him a hostile look. "I hate this. I need to be at the library. It cannot function without me there to properly maintain it."

"Do not worry. It will be fine. Please answer my question."

The Chief Fireman patted his mother's arm. "Don't worry, Mum, we won't be here much longer, will we Detective McBride?"

"I'm afraid that might not be possible."

"What!" Screamed the librarian.

"Figures! Can't trust no government lackeys," Mr. Warren snorted.

"Got homes to save," Chief Fireman blasted. "You cannot make us stay! You have no right!"

Inspector Dublin stood up. "Actually, Detective McBride does." He patted a folder he was holding meaningfully. "And there's an arrest warrant for murder resting peacefully here for when our little meeting is over."

The room broke into another chorus of anger and vitriol. Detective Margaret Mallory gave Scotch an amused look that said, "Fix this one!"

Scotch rolled his eyes, then took a ruler on the chalkboard base and slammed the flat of it so hard against the chalkboard it sent a cloud of chalk dust into the air and an explosion of sound like a bomb going off.

The room went silent as a tomb.

Scotch waited several moments, then sighed. "Truly, me thinks civilization has little hope at times like this, but I have a duty to be fair and logical. I intend to perform me duty to both functions perfectly. Now, will you please, all, remain silent unless spoken to."

The room remained silent but filled with a brooding, dark silence reeking of anger and resentment.

The librarian stared holes through Scotch and her son. Her son's eyes smoldered with disgust. Mr. Warren had no expression because he was nodding off to sleep.

Scotch gave the old man a look of deep compassion then said, "I think I can end this uncomfortable interrogation quite comfortably now."

He turned to Detective Margret Mallory, "Detective,

will you please kiss Mr. Warren on his forehead? Now.”

Detective Margaret Mallory gave Scotch a questioning look, almost defiant, but when he nodded to Inspector Dublin, the man cleared his throat. She then hurriedly rose and went round the table to kiss Mister Warren on his forehead.

The old man stirred but did not waken.

“Thank you. You may sit down again.”

She sat down and crossed her arms over her chest, defying Scotch to ask anything further of her.

He smiled.

The Chief Fireman gave his mother a questioning look. She ignored him.

Scotch cleared his throat. “Now, if I might, Madam,” he said to the librarian. “Would you please do the same?”

“Well, I never!” The librarian protested.

“Please,” Scotch said. “Indulge me.”

She hissed angrily, then got up and gave Old Man Warren a light kiss on his forehead.

Immediately, he stirred from his sleep as she went back to her seat. He said, “May!”

Scotch nodded to Inspector Dublin. He rose from his chair, took out a warrant and slapped it down on the table.

"Ms. Eleanor Berry Botham, I am serving you with a warrant for your arrest for the murder of Ms. May Mary Traymore! You have the right to remind silent, but anything you say now is admissible in court as evidence."

"I've done nothing wrong, Inspector."

"I do believe that Ms. May Mary Traymore might disagree with that statement."

"But she's dead!"

Inspector Dublin gave the librarian a dismissive look. 'Exactly."

The librarian jumped to her feet, shook a fist angrily at the Inspector. "You can't do this!"

"Oh, but I can, dear Ms. Botham. I most certainly can."

The Chief Fireman rose. "Mother, how could you do such a horrible thing?"

She gave him a shocked look.

Detective Margaret Mallory turned slightly and put out her left foot from beneath the table.

Inspector Dublin slapped a second warrant onto the tabletop. "And this is a warrant for your arrest for murder, Chief John Berry Botham."

The Chief made a dash for the door.

He made it hallway and then tripped on the foot of Detective Margaret Mallory.
She grinned as he tumbled to the floor, striking it so hard he let out a lungful of air.

Scotch gave her an appreciative nod, which she returned with a wink.

Inspector Dublin tapped the door and it opened to reveal four constables. "Please do escort the gentleman on the floor, and Ms. Botham to the holding cell, please."

He backed out of the way as the four broke up into pairs and lifted the Chief from the floor and stood next to Eleanor Botham, waiting for her to rise.

The constables escorted the two out of the room. Inspector Dublin shut the door and then turned to give the detectives a huge smile of relief.

"I must say, this has to have been the strangest way to uncover a murderer I've ever seen."

Scotch grinned. "Surely it didn't hurt any that you found samples of Ms. Traymore's DNA on the Chief's axe?"

Inspector Dublin nodded.

"Still, you must give more credit to Detective Mallory here. It is really, Margaret here who did the bulk of the work."

She glanced at Scotch. But said nothing.

"Well, be that as it may, I am sure that this pair is going to jail for a long, long time," Inspector Dublin said.

Scotch grinned. "And if God is merciful, the mother and son will share cells next to each other."

Margaret laughed. "Scotch, that's downright mean of you!"

2020 Rest and Relaxation

Scotch glanced at the building he was now living in. Otter no longer lived with him. He had left to live with his ailing mother, so now Scotch had the entire flat to himself. And tonight, he was glad that was so.

The air was a tad chilly. But tolerable.

A shake on his arm.

He gave Margaret, who had his arm in hers, a warm smile. "I feel reluctant to show you me new place."

"Oh, be reckless for once, McBride," she urged.

Then on his look, added. "But not too much!"

He laughed. "Now there speaks a woman who knows her limits."

She winked at him.

"You are so sure of that, are ye now?"

He laughed even harder.

She eyed the name over the entrance. "I wonder why they named this place Rest and Relaxation?"

"It used to be a center for the mentally challenged."

She smirked at him. "Well, then, you seem to have picked the perfect place to live."

They both laughed hard.

211B Rest and Relaxation

Margaret stood at the windows which looked out over Gloucester and sighed. "It's such a huge city, but at night all the concrete and dismal alleys fade into a pleasant shade of sparkling lights and dancing shadows."

"Which is precisely why I chose this place. It would drive Otter daffy were he still living here."

She turned to face Scotch as he entered the sitting room with two plates on a platter covered with a white cloth, silverware, and condiments.

"Breakfast is served."

She laughed. 'We have only been here an hour and you just cannot stop dropping hints, can you?"

He smirked at her. "Well, it takes a dirty mind to know one."

She barked with laughter and helped him set the table with the food. "We must do this more often, Scotch. Had I known you were such a good cook, I would have invited myself over sooner."

He laughed. "Well, if you can get used to having scrambled eggs for dinner, then I suppose it's a habit I could live with."

He frowned a moment.

She gave him a questioning look. "What's wrong?"

He helped her sit down, then sat opposite her. He poured tea for both, then leaned towards her, cupping his chin in his hands, and smiling.

"You look like an alligator about to swallow its victim," she accused.

"Alligators don't have whiskers and sideburns."

She reached across and rested her hand on his wrist. "Some. So, out with it."

"Sugar?" He asked, after taking some for himself.

She gave him a mischievous look. "Perhaps, later."

He grinned. "I was at Madame Crystal's earlier this week."

"Oh, that explains everything," she replied, spreading butter on her toast.

"Well, she brought up this strange image that has been bothering me since I left her."

"What image?"

"Scrambled eggs."

"No thanks. I already have plenty."

Scotch chuckled. "No, I meant she used those words to stir me up."

"Scrambled eggs?"

"Exactly."

Margaret eyed her scrambled eggs. "Premonition of our breakfast? Seems like a rather, uh, silly waste of a prediction, doesn't it?"

He took a bite of his toast and then nodded.

"Perhaps."

She drank some tea, watching his expression over the rim of her cup. "Oh, and why perhaps?"

Scotch explained. "When you told me about how a dead woman kissed Mr. Warren. It made me think."

Margaret set her cup down and waited.

"That the whole death thing seemed scrambled up...like eggs. Except if the whole thing stopped only with the kiss, it would have made no sense at all.'

"I sense your crystal ball is lighting up," Margaret teased.

"Not yet," he joked back.

She blushed.

He went on. "But once I knew about the librarian's relationship with her son, I did some digging of my own."

"How?"

"Cock."

"Ah! Him!"

Cock John Robin.

Scotch sat down at the usual chair Cock kept for his work and put a foot up, so Cock could begin polishing the shoe on it.

Cock got out his tools, then began polishing. Finished, Scotch put his other foot up.

Almost finished with the last shoe, Cock looked up with a smile. "Soon, it will be too late to ask," Cock urged.

Scotch leaned forward. "I'm puzzled by a case I'm handling at the moment."

"Don't be."

"Why not?"

Cock finished Scotch's last shoe, then looked up. He studied Scotch a moment, rubbed his shock of hair a further moment, then said. "Scrambled eggs take more than one egg to be made right."

Then Cock got up, with his tools and walked away.

"Wait!" Scotch cried out. "I haven't paid you yet!"

Cock ignored him and vanished into the crowds walking past.

211B Rest and Relaxation

"That man sure knows how to scramble a person's brains, doesn't he?"

Scotch took Margaret's hands in his and squeezed them. "On the contrary, it was my thoughts that were scrambled eggs, because I had been trying to make one add up to two all along and hadn't realized it yet."

"And?" Margaret asked sweetly, squeezing his hands in return.

"Why would the librarian kiss Mister Warren's forehead while he slept? It made no sense, unless…"

"Unless what?"

Scotch sighed. "Two were involved in the murder. The one who murdered May, and the one who tried to cover it up."

"Mother and son."

"Exactly," Scotch replied with a grin.

Margaret thought about it for a long time, finishing her scrambled eggs and toast. Scotch waited, finishing his as well.

Finally, she looked at him again. "I think I can see what glued your eggs together finally.'

"Please enlighten me."

So, she did.

"Jealousy can drive a person sometimes to do truly heinous things."

"And a son who hates his mother but will do anything to please her..." Scotch ventured.

Margaret smiled. "...Would be the perfect partner in crime. He would kill May and..."

"The mother would confuse the issue by pretending through the kiss that May had been alive when she was not."

"Giving our Mr. Warren no reason to suspect that his old sweetheart, had anything to do with the crime."

Margaret laughed. "And providing a proper alibi for her and her son."

Scotch nodded. "My, we are becoming quite the pair, are we not??"

Margaret smiled. "That old crystal ball of yours is getting better and better."

Scotch rose. "Then perhaps I should see what more it can do for me."

Margaret rose as well. "That sounds like a wonderful idea."

Scotch gave her a surprised look. "Really?"

"Oh, I never leave a man guessing my thoughts. That

would be so unkind."

Scotch gave her another surprised look.

Margaret headed around the table towards him, but instead of stopping, she went to the coatrack by the door and reached for her coat and hat.

He burst into laughter as she said, "Therefore, I'd best be off before I do so."

Scotch opened the door for her to leave.

"One more thing, Scotch."

"Yes."

She turned to face him. "You agreed with my statement that she had been jealous. But I did not say of who or what!"

Scotch grinned. "I did a bit of research after the vault fiasco."

"And?"

"It occurred to me to have a wee bit of a talk with Mr. Warren to help clarify some things."

"Oh."

"It seems that the old man, God bless his soul, once dated the librarian, but then dumped her when he discovered her true nature."

"Thank you," Margaret said.

She started to exit, then on impulse turned about and gave him a quick kiss on his cheek. "Maybe next time?"

"Dare I ask what?"

She laughed and began making her way down the staircase.

"Maybe. Maybe, not," he said softly as he shut his door.

GHOST ISLAND

Table of Contents

The Cold Room

Scotland Yard

Glasgow, Scotland

Early Morning

Hans "Otter" Franklin eyed the slab of steel that the departed female lay upon, a canvas sheet pulled across her privates and breasts. She had to have been quite the looker in her younger days.

But Midnight Angels, he sighed inwardly, they do not usually have anything but...so many of them are found dead, strangled, throats slit or tossed in the waters to drown.

Women who sold their bodies for a living were not well respected in Glasgow or anywhere else for that matter, because they were women first and sellers of flesh last.

And women in a man's world did not fare as well as they might in a world of equality.

Otter, nicknamed by his friend standing next to him, Detective Scotch McBride, was tall, thickly built, with large, muscled arms, but a delicate face as prone to laughter as to deeper thought.

His eyes are German blue and of course can stare holes through your soul.

A complex man, who has never married, or even considered it of late. Content to be Scotch's companion in solving crimes. Bit rounded in the waist. Loves celery like some like sweets. But if that is the only fault a man has, then he must be close to being a saint, or at least a man you would not fear to meet in the dark.

Scotch appraised his friend a moment thoughtfully, then returned his attention to the corpse on the slab. The vertical stitching was all that remained of the violation of this woman's flesh. Her first violation had been the way she died.

Otter watched his friend with interest. He had his own opinion of how this Midnight Angel had expired but kept it to himself. Scotch would reach out to him if he felt something missing in his examination.

Otter watched silently as Scotch McBride did his perusal of the woman's shape, referring to notes left by the M.E., Medical Examiner for him.

Scotch McBride is Scottish with a bit of a brogue. Soft mannered. Easy going. Slow to make a judgement, but quick on the clues once he has them. Blondish hair and days old beard. Head cocks to the right most of the time.

As tall as Otter, but wiry with a strength not at once visible to look upon him.

His handsome, roguish face was as apt to break into a grin as a frown when he was at work. Confusing to his suspects and equally as confusing to the constables and Inspector who hired him to work.

His beard was never full. Always looked like it was as ready to leap from his face as to grow there was his trademark.

"Well, nasty bit, I would think, Detective McBride."

Scotch looked to the owner of the voice, Sir Flim O'Brien. M.E. (Medical Examiner) for the Yard. Affects a Sherlock Holmes type of persona with the same type of pipe, cloak, and hat when he is able.

Now he is not wearing the cloak or hat but is holding a pipe. But unlit. Yard procedure did not allow smoking in the Cold Room. Nor would Flim have ever disobeyed the rules. He knew how precise criminal forensics had to be and any kind of scent, smoke or otherwise that could change the nature of the victim's demise could be catastrophic to any evidence looked for.

"Being strangled to death by a fish is never a happy way to die."

Otter shook his head. "Why would anyone even think of such a horrid thing? A whole fish shoved into her windpipe." He shook his head again. His sadness almost overwhelming.

He knew the woman had no loved ones left behind.

Sometimes they had family they were supplying shelter and food for, but this one was a longer. A kind person from every interview he and Scotch had been upon.

Scotch nodded his agreement. Looked at Flim. "I agree. And the fishmonger who did this shall soon regret his mistake."

Flim gave Scotch a curious glance.

Scotch elaborated. He pointed to the woman's gaping mouth and the parts of her jaw that distended outwards. "The man who did this was abnormally strong. He broke her jaw on both sides, upper and lower to force the fish down her throat and block her air passage."

He looked to Flim, who gave him an encouraging nod.

"Furthermore," Scotch continued, "The killer used a size ten fishhook made of tainted iron to haul her over the waters to drop."

Detective Margaret Mallory, a female detective, steps from the side of Flim and gives Scotch a cool glance. "That is an exceptionally large leap in logic, Detective McBride.

Scotch grins, which causes her to flinch. He never does that unless he is about to hammer you into dust with his logic.

He is patient and waits for her emotions to calm down. She tends to be impulsive and rush into conclusions that are inadequate to the evidence.

She and he have been friends, but there is a lingering touch of something else between them, which he has not quite analyzed successfully yet. Perhaps because she is much like the modern cool boxes that become very warm suddenly or quite cold if not working properly.

Younger by about five years with a soft complexion, part Irish, part Scotch and bright as the new Tesla-Edison lightbulbs now spreading across Scotland. She had a wonderful sense of humor when she allowed it. A brilliant mind. And the scent of sandalwood and roses fragrance behind her right ear.

She is a fine-looking young woman with a brisk chin, spotty freckles, proud nose, startling eyes set like rose petals beneath a warm brow of radiance, and a pale complexion.

"Detective!"

Scotch flicked his eyes back to Flim. "Sorry, I lost my train of thought for a moment."

Otter and Detective Mallory exchanged brief looks. They both knew why, but neither would say it aloud.

"Not at all, Detective Mallory," Scotch explained. He rubbed his itchy beard a long moment in thought, then took a small wooden pointer and used its tip to gently pry the canvas sheet down the woman's body.

Detective Mallory grimaced.

"This," Scotch explained, touching the tip of the pointer to a long tear in the woman's abdomen. "This, if you had said fishhook now, would be just the correct width of tear made when a fish tried to break free."

Detective Mallory had seen and heard too much. A young detective still, it was more than she could handle. Fortunately for her and for the others, Otter offered her a silver bowl to toss in.

She took it, hurried to the back of the room, and tossed her guts up.

Loudly.

Awareness of Inspector Dublin's entrance into the Cold Room came with a surge of unexpected warm air across everyone, then it vanished once he closed the heavy door to the Cold Room.

He spotted the tear in the Midnight Angel's abdomen and grimaced. "I say, rather nasty cut to her belly. Poor soul. That must have been a wretched way to die!"

Detective Mallory began a new series of tossing her guts into the silver bowl. Otter quickly went over and gave her a new one.

She nodded gratefully, then began filling the new one as a fresh series of spasms quaked her guts.

Inspector Dublin eyed her dubiously.

Scotch took the Inspector's arm and guided him towards the exit. "I have a theory I'd like to go over with you."

"Good. And I also have a new case for you."

"I hope it's not as bizarre as this one."

The Inspector paused at the door. "May I be frank?"

"Please."

"You are going to hate this job."

Scotch gave the Inspector a close glance, shrugged, then opened the door out. A fresh blast of stifling air struck the two as they exited.

Detective Mallory sat the second silver bowl down next a sink and gripped its sides. Weakly, she said. "Otter, why do I always disgrace myself so utterly at times such this?"

Otter smiled. "I tossed my guts all over Scotch the first time he showed me a corpse like this."

She eyed him uncertainly. "Really?

"Yes."

"Does it ever stop?"

"Yes."

"Good," she said with a sigh. She straightened, reached for a dry towel, and began wiping her mouth and face. "Good," she repeated.

"But my dreams are not the same anymore."

Detective Mallory stiffened.

Otter recovered the dead Midnight Angel, muttered a soft prayer over her body and headed for the door.

Laura's Song

"Darlings play in the waves
Singing songs soft and brave.
Hardly moving with a sound
Their toes gliding above the ground.
Dolly plays with them nice
Fishy tails and eyes so bright
They call to her in voices sweet
Come swim with us deep beneath."

Fisherman Sean Monnery

Sean, a tall man, squeezed into a small sailing craft, shifted oars, set his fishing gear in a box, then tossed his mooring line to the hard rock next him.

The waters tossed his boat up and down gently as he rose to step across and tie his boat to shore. Fingal's Cave was a work of art.

Nature's art.

It stretched upwards for dozens of yards. Its face spread across dozens more yards. Rocks piled atop each other in a symmetrical pattern greeted his eyes whether he looked up or down.

He did a slip knot over the stanchion pounded into the small slip of rock that fronted the right side of the cave. Then he eyed the narrow path that thrust eagerly into the depths of the cave.

He reached back into his boat and retrieved an oil lantern. He lifted its lens, then struck a wooden match on the rock face and lit its wick. He slid the glass back into place, then entered the cave.

The water streaming through its center chuckled and sang its maritime tune. The one he had just finished singing before he moored his craft. It was an old tune. A sad tune. A seaman's ditty. A remembrance of the lost souls found here over the years.

Today, he had no fear of finding anything, but the small case of spirits he had tucked away several dozen yards inside. His wife had been nagging him over his drinking so much of late, he had sworn to never touch another drop in the house again.

And he had kept his promise. By moving his spirits to this place. It was so frightening to the citizens of his village that none ventured here but him. He smiled as he neared the objects of his desire.

He took a slight turn, held his oil lantern higher

"Ahhh!" He sighed with pleasure.

He saw the crate with is sprits. But then he squinted against the glare of his lantern. What was that hanging over the top of his crate.

It looked like. Like…

As he came closer, he saw exactly what it was.

A man should never scream in fear.

His scream was not in fear!

Nor did it last a long time.

But seagulls who were nesting along the face of Fingal's Cave all shot into the air in a blur, their cries of fear matching that of Sean's.

Grief

Angus McGree did not know whether to sit next his wife and hold her close, or to shake his fist at the heavens and demand justice. His rage poured into two jars now. One his pride. The other his sorrow.

Pride his daughter will be remembered.

Grief and anger that she is not here for him to hold and cherish.

"And I tell you right here and now, as God be my witness, that I shall hunt down the killer of my daughter until my last breath is gone if need be."

The entire village rose as one and broke into applause.

His weeping wife stopped.

He gaped at all the friends, family and loved ones he knew in the audience. Even strangers were here. Not one person was missing.

He could go on no further.

He wanted to.

He needed to.

But his own internal fire had now exploded into a volcanic eruption inside his chest. He clutched at his heart, his eyes rolled up in his head.

He collapsed on the small stage, folding into himself and a comforting darkness briefly lit by an opening door of pure white light.

The first to reach his side and glance into his face saw a man with grief no longer upon his face. They saw a smile in his eyes.

The man crossed himself. "He is with his daughter now in heaven."

Scotch and Otter exchanged glances. Otter crossed himself. Scotch grit his teeth, fresh determination lighting his features.

He rose to leave.

Detective Mallory rose next, then Otter.

"What now?" Detective Mallory asked.

"We find the bastard who murdered the child and the father!"

"But only the child was murdered," protested Detective Mallory.

Scotch looked into her eyes. "You don't really believe that do you?"

He turned away to leave. "Wait!" He turned back. "Yes?"

"Are you off to have all your man fun while I get stuck here doing the dirty work again?"

Scotch gave Otter a roll of the eyes, then left without another word.

Detective Mallory touched Otter's arm. "Is he always like this?"

Otter smiled. "Always."

"But where is he going. Fingal's Island is not that way."

Otter laughed. "You will figure it out. Come. We have to secure a place to stay and maybe a bite to eat."

"I'm not hungry."

Otter gave her a look she had never seen before and shrugged. "Have it your way then. But you will be. You will be."

Ghost Island

"It's been named properly as Fingal's Island, but because of the recurring tragedies it's been secretly called Ghost Island," Father McKiernen explained to the passenger in his boat.

Scotch scratched at his beard, saying nothing. He eyed the approaching cave that swept deep into the island. The perfectly shaped columns of rock were fantastic to the eye. Amazing how nature could have created this shape. It was almost surreal. How had it been constructed by nature to look so human made? Perhaps, legends of Merlin creating this enigmatic cave were true.

He smiled at that thought. Merlin had always been his favorite story book character. His father would make these wonderful drawings of Merlin. Merlin was a gentle, soft expression of pencil that lit up the paper it was on. Not one harsh or dark line described his face. Always, his expression was gentle, but firm. Kind, but powerfully directed to do the right thing.

In ways, Scotch fancied himself as a Merlin of sorts, working the magic of forensics science to convert a murder into justice, a theft into a solution.

Some legends claimed the island had been created by Merlin the Magician. To honor the loss of the Great King Arthur. Merlin's grief, rather than lashing out to destroy and plunder, as many another lord of name might have in those days looked for a different more constructive direction to give his grief an outlet. He, instead, had used his powerful Earth Magic to layer this island like a brick layer...layer by layer by layer.

"Mister McBride?"

"Sorry, my mind drifted back to my childhood for a moment. Merlin was always an important part of my youth."

"God should be the most important part!" Father McKiernan scolded Scotch.

Scotch chose to ignore the scathing reply. "Well then," Scotch admitted coyly. "It would seem the island has a rather prominent place in the history of your village then."

"Too much."

"How so?" Scotch asked, his eyes now on his companion, who was steering the steam driven boat...a four-seater...with paddlewheels aft and a prow braced by two angels, carved delicately from some kind reddish wood Scotch was unfamiliar with.

Father McKiernen scowled a moment. Obviously, the subject was distasteful to the man, but he sighed finally and relented to speak. "This is the thirteenth in as many years."

He looked Scotch directly in the eyes. "All children."

Father McKiernan clenched his right hand into a fist. "This monster is killing our angels! It must stop!"

Scotch did not react. He already knew the answer.

He turned to his companion, Detective Margaret Mallory.

Younger by about five years with a soft complexion, part Irish, part Scotch and bright as a lightbulb, with a good sense of humor and a sharp mind. Detective Margaret as Scotch liked to call her affectionately, wore the usual sandalwood and roses fragrance behind her right ear.

It was noticeable because of the odd combination. Plus, it was strong.

Many a night after work he had fancied what it would be like to put his lips there.

She caught the look in his eyes and looked away, a gentle smile caressing her lips. She was a fine-looking young woman with a brisk chin, freckle spots, proud nose, startling eyes set like rose petals beneath a warm brow of radiance, and a pale complexion.

He was amazed she decided to take the hot ride with him. She had related to him earlier she got seasick easily. But she had showed up, smiling and eager to go. So, he had nothing further to say. She had been in charge. So be it. A woman had as much right as a man to be stubborn and reckless. He felt too much affection towards her to judge her for these aspects of her.

"The sun is not her friend," Otter would often remind Scotch when Scotch spoke of Detective Mallory's freckles affectionately."

Scotch rubbed his jaw, as if thinking deeply over the father's words, but he was not. Instead, his mind and thoughts were on Otter, who was aft gobbling down slices of home-made bread the father's cook had made for their passage. He could also smell it. It made his mouth water. The cook was excellent and had spiced the bread with cinnamon and cloves. He had a sweet tooth for anything cinnamon, but Otter had an addiction to it, judging how quickly he was imbibing the bread that moment.

Detective Margaret glanced at Father McKiernan. "Aye and I would suspect that the stigma of Ghost Island is likely to become embedded in its history even deeper than the legend of Merlin and King Arthur."

She gave Scotch a side glance, showing him how easy it was to read his thoughts.

Scotch arched an eyebrow in response, and she pulled on her right ear, showing she was aware of that thought as well.

He blushed.

Turned back to Father McKiernen. "I agree." Scotch felt his neck burn from Detective Mallory's stare at him

She chuckled. They rarely agreed, which is why she had gone with him, more than likely. He had been very heady about the trip not being a woman's job. Too dangerous.

She had laughed him off. And he knew then she would come despite her fears, rather than admit the journey terrified her.

He both respected her for her determination and worried about her deepest motives. But that did not need considering currently. Maybe, never. Maybe, she was really a reflection of his own stubbornness and determination.

Madame Crystal said once to him that all we met in our lives were reflections of part of us. To not judge them harshly, or we would be sentencing our own self as well.

The steamboat's engine chuckled to a slow stop as Father McKiernen powered it down. The small craft drifted slowly next to the carved landing at the mouth of the cave on Ghost Island.

"Here we be," he said, a sad tone to his voice. Cracking partially, as if he might burst into tears.

He glanced at Detective Margaret. She offered him a handkerchief and he took it, wiped his tears away and blew his nose. "I'll give you a fresh one when we return to the village," he promised her.

She did not reply. She would not use it again anyway. Something about the idea repulsed her.

He nodded, then cast a rope expertly about a stanchion poking up from the lip of the landing. It landed perfectly over the stanchion and tightened below the two huge bolts at the stanchion's head.

"Well, off we go then."

Otter hurriedly gulped down another slice of buttered bread, then came awkwardly along the side of the steamboat, stepping over cradles of rope, buckets of miscellaneous items, until he joined Scotch.

"It's an ugly place," Otter commented.

"It wasn't always," Father McKiernen replied.

He looked away, as if seeing something in the distance. "It wasn't always."

Scotch and Detective Margaret exchanged glances.

Not lost on Otter, who noted the intensity of them, then looked away.

"After you, Father," Scotch said.

He helped the Father disembark, then offered Detective Margaret a hand. She ignored it and leaped nimbly across the narrow gap of water from boat to landing. She grinned at him.

Scotch remained impersonal to her obvious rejection, and instead turned to Otter. "Someone has to mind the boat."

"In case of?" His friend asked.

"Exactly."

Father McKiernen did not notice. He was already slipping the cave opening, carefully working his way into the darkness.

Otter reached back to an oil lamp at the side, lit it with a stick match, and handed it to Scotch. "You might need this."

Scotch laughed. "Ever the optimist, Otter, aren't ye me lad?"

"I've had a great teacher."

Scotch grinned, patted his friend on the shoulder, then also leaped to the landing.

He glanced at Detective Margaret. "Shall we?"

"I shall," she responded, taking the lamp away from him and entering immediately ahead of him.

Otter broke into laughter.

Scotch glanced at his friend. "It could be worse."

"Not by much," Otter replied with a chuckle.

Scotch cursed beneath his breath and hurried to catch up with Detective Margaret. This dratted woman seemed intent on embarrassing him and outmanning him at every turn. Part of him loved her for that independence, and another part chafed, feeling used.

He caught his thoughts into a neat bundle and tossed them into the stream rushing out the cave and hurried along.

Angus McGree

"Father, I will be late for dinner."

"No problem, Tennifer."

She gave Angus's gruff face a quick kiss. He smiled despite himself and returned to working on the wagon he was repairing.

Tennifer had the grace of a cat, the stature of a Fairie and a name she had made up for herself. Smart from birth, she was one who never needed to instructions repeated to her.

A miracle child, Father McKiernen had called her.

She was short yes, but because of her unique name and her wonderfully sweet and benevolent nature, loved by everyone. She was a ball of laughter and energy, spritely, lovely in every sense of the word. Four feet of laughter, smiles and feminine youth. She surely descended from the Fairie of legend. Though Angus could not, for the world of him, figure out how that could have happened, since he never slept with any of the Fay. She brought so much delight to everyone with her peals of silver laughter. Her impish smile. Her readiness to help at the drop of a hat.

Not much more than ten years old. She was long

limbed, lithe as a willow tree, and strong as a young ox. She was the boy Angus had wished for, but not gotten. Still. She was pretty and had a warm personality that everyone who knew her loved. And he got over his desire for a boy instead and feasted on her wonderfully kind and sweet nature.

She was Angus's pride and joy, but unfortunately for him, then and later, he could spend little time with her. His hours were brutally long and horribly wearing on his aging body. At forty, he was close to the oldest man of the village, except for Father McKiernen. The Father was pushing thirty and kept a straight back and black hair.

Ah, the miracles of science, Angus thought fondly. Even a man of God can be old before his time, but Father McKiernan managed to keep his boyish ways and disposition long after most men his age were ready to retire and rock a chair until it broke.

He laughed at the image and returned to prying a nail loose that was catching on one of the cogs of a wheel that had loosened and rose to snag several floorboards and hole them with spreading cracks, like the ground being opened a massive shaking from below.

Molly, Molly, Dear Molly

Molly Wagoner set down her knitting as a lightning bolt of pink flesh and girlish laughter greeted her with warm arms about her neck and a quick kiss on her right cheek, and then the left.

"Morning, Molly, Molly, Dear Molly!" Tennifer laughed.

Molly set down the sweet young child and smiled broadly at her, showing her two missing front teeth. "And to you, my dear."

"I've got something for you," Tennifer said. She pulled a large red apple from a bag she had been carrying and handed it over.

Molly's eyes widened. "Oh, but it's so big!"

Tennifer grinned happily. "Biggest!"

Molly set the large red apple atop her yarn and looked Tinner straight in the eyes. "I swear you are an angel in disguise."

"I am, I am, I am!" Tennifer replied, jumping up and down to the beat of the words.

"Bye Tennifer!"

"Bye Molly!" Tennifer grabbed her bag again, hefted it over her right shoulder and took off in a series of leaps and bounds. She called it her cat leap. She loved cats and watched their every move. Part of the reason she was so nimble, besides age, was that she copied the way they stretched and moved.

Molly had heard that aged men in the Indias contorted their bodies like that to stay youthful and supple. She believed it. Tennifer was a prime example of how nimble a body could be.

Molly got up, took the apple Tennifer had gifted her and went inside her humble home. It was quite small. But more than enough for her to handle. She went into a semi-lit kitchen, filled with oblong shadows cast by the rising sun as it moved towards that side of her home. The light caroused through make-shift windows she had constructed in her youthful days.

She opened a pantry door and set the big red apple next to a big green apple showing signs of yellowing. It sat next another apple that was completely yellow. Then another which was shriveling, its skin tightening and turning crisp and dry.

In all she had at least two dozen apples on display. Each one a day older than the one next it.

She gazed lovingly at the apples, a touch of sadness on her lips. She could not bear to tell Tennifer that with her two front teeth and the rest of her teeth rotting in her mouth, she had no way to eat anything but liquids these days.

She opened another cabinet door and revealed a jar of milk. It was curdling.

She sighed and reached for it. It tasted horrible. But it was food.

Church of God

Father McKiernan knelt before a statue of Jesus, with a smiling face and upraised arms. Head bowed, he prayed. "Dear Father in heaven, let me be your humble servant in all things and forgive me trespasses even as I forgive those of others."

He raised his head at the sound of entering feet. Smiled. "Amen!"

"Father!" Tennifer laughed as much as said, as she flew down the short aisle to wrap her arms about his neck.

He rose at once and twirled her around.

She screamed with delight.

He set her down and nodded towards the door to the right of Jesus. "I've got a really big surprise for you today, Tennifer."

She took his right hand. "Show me! Show me! Show me!"

"You sure? It is going to be much bigger than the last surprise I gave you."

Her eyes widened with happiness. "Oh! Bigger! Yes. Yes. Yes."

He smiled and led her towards the door.

The Constabulary

"I'm sorry we haven't much comfort to offer," Constable McHawkins said in a calm voice.

He motioned Scotch and Otter to a small room with a large table, and four chairs. The room was semi-lit with candle scones that cast soft, flickering light.

"No power?"

"Never had power. Probably never will," Constable McHawkins said apologetically.

"No problem, Constable," Scotch said. "I realize you are a small village with little means.

"Just getting you to come here to help with the investigation has been a great expense to our small village."

"I can imagine," Scotch replied, eyeing the beat-up chairs.

He sat in one. "Otter, please admit those who wish to make a statement as soon as the one prior has left.

Otter nodded. And went to the outside of the small conference room to wait for the first witness.

Constable McHawkins looked flustered. "These are not suspects, Detective McBride. I hope you understand that!"

"I do. And I will not abuse your kindness."

"Very well then. Your first visitor should arrive in about five minutes."

The constable left. Then returned. "Shall I have Detective Mallory enter once she arrives?"

Scotch nodded yes.

The constable nodded and turned to leave. As he did, Scotch noticed that the man's right index finger was twitching. "I will instruct your man...?"

"Otter."

"Otter as to the list of witnesses."

"You won't be waiting here?"

"I have a pressing business at the other end of the village."

Scotch frowned a moment. "Very well. Please do."

The constable exited and spoke quietly to Otter several moments, then hurried away.

Otter looked inside and gave Scotch a wink.

Scotch smiled. Good, reliable Otter.

A tall man brushed past Otter, causing Otter to stumble. The tall man entered the room without an apology. He had a dark face and piercing green eyes. "I be McCarthy."

The man had multiple scars on his right hand.

Scotch frowned a moment, then rose to shake hands. "Detective Scotch McBride." He gestured to the chair opposite him. "Please, Mister McCarthy, have a seat."

"This better not be long; I have better things to do than sit here all morning."

Scotch arched an eyebrow. That is when he noticed the man had a deep scratch mark recently healed on the right side of his thick neck.

Scotch frowned deeply a moment.

The man scowled at him in return. "Well, be on with your foolishness!"

"Why is that Mister McCarthy?"

Mister McCarthy leaned forward across the table, glanced at the open doorway, as if searching for someone, then whispered. "Because I know who the killer is!"

Scotch's eyes widened.

"Truly then?"

The tall man crossed his heart and rolled his eyes to heaven. "Truly, as the great Lord is in heaven."

Scotch opened his notebook, dipped his quill in a small inkwell bottle, then waited.

"Please enlighten me."

The tall man smiled, his face creasing with self-satisfaction. "Father McKiernen."

"Oh? And why do you say that?"

The tall man leaned forward once more, glanced out the door again. "Because everyone knows the priest has a thing for young girls."

Scotch stopped writing and looked up.

"Truly then?"

"As the Lord is my witness, I swear that be so."

The Tall Man

Mister McCarthy looked in both directions as he exited the small building. Down the street an old man sat sleeping with a blanket over his lap in the morning sun. He was the proprietor of a small tobacco shop.

Further along, two older women sat on rocking chairs, knitting back stockings for babies that would never be born. Tennifer had been the last child born in their village.

The small pub, the center of civilization for this humble village, sat square in the middle of the village as well. Thick smoke drifted over its double doors, swirling in curtains of gray and white.

The curls of smoke rose over the top of the doors and gently wafted skywards towards glowing clouds that extended wispy arms towards a sun soon to sleep in the arms of night's embrace.

Mister McCarthy glanced sharply behind him once, as if someone were there. There was not.

He continued to the end of the village and then passed from view as he prepared to take a turn past the last structure, a small grocer. The grocer sat on the porch, whittling away at a large bone, shaping it into an animal not resolved enough yet to figure out its kind.

"Mister McCarthy."

"Rufus!" Mister McCarthy spoke back as he vanished from view to the side of the building.

Rufus put his knife away, set down his carving. Locked his shop, stuck his hands in his thick, woolen britches, then whistling, headed for his appointment at the constabulary.

Rufus's Confession

Scotch eyed Rufus sternly as the man rubbed vigorously at his thick sideburns, which clung to his face like a pair of inverted chipmunk tails, thick and red. He stopped and eyed Scotch with watery blue eyes. "I know who murdered the dear little child."

Scotch glanced at his notepad. It had a list of thirty names now. All with checkmarks beside them. He had stopped taking notes a long time ago.

"Truly?"

"Indeed!"

Scotch nodded, leaned forward. "Enlighten me."

Rufus did. "Mister McCarthy!"

Scotch rose and offered his hand. "Very good, sir. I be thanking ye for your confidence."

Rufus gave Scotch a confused look. "Don't you want to even know why I know this?"

Scotch pretended to be reading his notes, nodding his head vigorously, mumbling unintelligently beneath his breath, then looked up. He shut the notebook and smiled. "No. I am quite relieved in fact that you have been so helpful. Have a good evening, sir."

Rufus nodded and exited.

Otter peeked inside. He arched an eyebrow questioningly.

"Is our last witness here yet?"

"She is, Scotch."

Otter stepped aside and Molly Waggoner walked past him.

The Last Witness

Molly Waggoner sat as still as a stone; her eyes glazed over. Tears streaking her face. Hands folded in her lap, as if waiting for prayers to begin.

Scotch gazed at her from across the conference table, his eyes fixed on her posture a moment, then the veins in her neck, then the angle at which she sat upon her hardwood chair.

The constable had been right. The village was poor. Not a single chair in the building was in good condition. His had a hole in the right side that cut at his bottom. He was quite sure that Molly's was the only good chair, but it looked as if it had seen much, much better days.

And his bottom was beginning to wear out quite as much as his patience at this moment. He had few remaining hopes as to this witness. But being the normally patient detective, he nodded to Molly.

He leaned forward. "When was the last time you saw Tennifer, Missus Waggoner?"

She wiped at tears clinging to her pale cheeks, then leaned forward. "Why don't we cut to the chase, Detective McBride."

"Very well. So, we shall. You know who did it?"

"I do."

"And...?

"Constable McHawkins killed dear sweet, Tennifer."

Molly could hold back no longer. She broke into a tsunami of tears and sobs.

Scotch leaned back on his chair. Shifting slightly to ease the ache in his bottom, which reminded him yet again of pressing matters.

But not so much that he did not notice certain aspects of Molly's appearance.

His eyebrows rose as he finished contemplating her.

He stood up. "Please, we are through now. I am sorry to have brought you so much grief, Missus Wagoner. It is an unpleasant job I have to do."

She rose. "I appreciate your kind words, Detective."

She gave him a brief smile. Then she spit out, "I hope that Constable McHawkins roasts his soul in hell for taking that dear child's life!"

She whisked past Otter.

Scotch waited, until the sound of her footsteps faded, then eclipsed by the sound of the front door of the constabulary shutting, then cleared his throat.

Otter entered; a questioning look on his face.

"We have a problem, Otter."

"We do?"

"Yes. I need you to carry a message for me to London."

"What will you do in the meanwhile?"

Scotch frowned a moment, then sat down. "Ouch!" He got back up and rubbed his bottom. "Put ointment on my sore ass is what I will do."

Otter chuckled.

The Cove Hostelry

Scotch sighed wearily as he approached the entrance to the old hostelry. It was to be his residence for the next few…he hoped…days. But more than likely it would be longer. In cases like this one, time was of the essence and could just as easily be your friend as your enemy.

As he reached for the door, Detective Mallory opened it and came out. She looked even more weary than he felt. She had dark circles under her eyes. Her makeup was non-existent, which told him she had indeed been quite busy.

"Well?" She inquired.

"Well?" He replied with a slight grin.

She gave him a grim look.

He nodded. Sighed. "I feared so."

Fingal's Island

"And this is where the fisherman, Mister Monnery found her body?" Scotch asked.

"It is," Father McKiernan replied.

Detective Mallory set the oil lamp on a high shelving of rock, also geometrically shaped as all the other rocks all the way back to the outside. It creeped her out. The dankness, gloom, and pallor of her companions. She felt as if she were in the middle of one of Edgar Allan Poe's horror tales.

Scotch nodded.

His nostrils flared briefly at a familiar scent in the air. He smiled. Good!

He turned to Father McKiernen. "Very well. We are through here then."

He folded his hands behind his back and headed for the entrance.

"That's it?" Father McKiernan demanded, refusing to budge.

Scotch turned about and frowned at Father McKiernen. "Unless you have something you wish to confide to us, Father McKiernen. Yes."

Father McKiernen looked stricken a moment, then shook his head.

Scotch continued for the exit to the caves, the sound of rushing water echoing in the tight passageway.

Detective Mallory and Otter exchanged glances, then followed.

Neither Scotch nor Father McKiernen had any problem finding their way back. Which bothered Detective Mallory to no end. She had to talk with that man later when they returned to the Cove Hostelry. Scotch was being closer fisted than usual and that frightened her. Why? She could not put a finger on it. Just a premonition.

Shaking her head, she hurried to catch up.

Otter followed her; his thoughts lost in directions that might have surprised her had she known.

It was going to be a long boat trip home. Exceedingly long. For all of them.

Village Meeting

Scotch waited until the last person entered the large hall. It seated the entire village. About a hundred people. They all stared at him. Some yawned. Some had brought knitting. Some food. Some chessboards and checkers.

Scotch nodded to Father McKiernen as he shut the door behind him.

He walked past two strangers seated in the rear of the hall, their faces lost in the shadows of flickering oil lamps.

No electricity meant most were in bed by this time. But Scotch could not wait until the morning. Duty pressed and he was determined to bring the case to a close.

When Father McKiernen sat at the front right side, Scotch nodded to him. "Thanks for joining us, Father McKiernen."

Father McKiernen nodded with satisfaction. "I would have it no other way. Justice must be served."

"Indeed, it must, Father," Scotch agreed with a wisp of a smile on his face.

He glanced to the rear where Detective Mallory was chatting quietly with the two strangers. Scotch noted the cape and hat on the taller and the pipe clutched in his right hand. He glanced at the shorter man, who was rubbing his stomach, as if it hurt him.

Otter cleared his throat.

The hint was obvious.

Time.

Scotch took a small gavel of the podium before him and struck it several times.

The small crowd shifted uneasily several moments, then settled down, all eyes on him.

Scotch glanced at the two men in back. The taller one nodded to Scotch with his pipe.

Scotch smiled. Returned his attention to the villagers. "I wish to say yet once more it is with the deepest of regrets that I have carried out this assignment. I've had many an unusual case in my life. But surely the loss of such a sweet child, beloved by all, is perplexing as well as touching to me."

He paused, feeling himself choke up for a moment, then he continued. Detective Mallory gave him a surprised look, then hid her face in the shadows again.

Scotch did not notice. His thoughts were a tornado of fear, doubt, and confusion. Yet at the same time…a certainty that put the very fear of God in his soul. But not because he had done anything wrong. But because…

He spoke. "I have determined who the killer is."

The villagers broke into chatter. Some angry. Some disgusted. Some clapped for him. Others rose and raised fists.

Scotch raised his hands and the Villagers settled down again.

"It is one of the darkest moments of my short life that I have to announce who the killer is."

Another disturbance of equal proportions stirred the crowd, but this time they settled more quickly and leaned forward in anticipation. Tired eyes. Sad eyes. Weeping eyes. Angry eyes. All eyes fixed on Scotch.

"Otter!" Scotch said quietly.

Otter rose and headed for the exit in back.

Scotch waited until he had shut the door, then spoke again.

"As you know it's been a long and grueling two weeks as I drew this case to a close."

Rufus grunted. He sat near the back. He rose to leave. "About time too. A man, can at last, find a night of peaceful rest, knowing a killer is no longer loose in his village."

"Please do be seated, Mister McCarthy."

Rufus made growing sounds deep in his throat but sat down again. He scowled at Scotch.

Molly, seated front row, stood up. "I demand you tell us now so we can bring closure to this horrible event."

She began crying again. Sobbing, she said, "It's breaking my heart all over again, thinking of that poor child, murdered so cruelly."

Scotch nodded at her. "Please, be seated. I am almost done."

She sat down.

Father McKiernan stood up suddenly. "God demands punishment for the cruelty! Who killed the lass?"

Everyone jumped to their feet, raising fists, and yelling for justice.

A gunshot from the back of the hall.

Everyone froze in place.

Scotch smiled warmly. "Please forgive my friend for shocking you, but I was about to reveal the answer to your question. Please be seated."

Everyone sat down again.

Scotch leaned against the podium.

Detective Mallory was looking at him. He gave her a smile, then the back door opened. Otter stood framed in it. He nodded.

Scotch sighed with relief, then said, "It is not often that legends have some element of truth to them."

Father McKiernen shifted uncomfortably on his chair.

"But when so much of fact is exposed, one must definitely give the nod to its veracity."

Rufus glanced nervously around.

"Fairie, as many of you know, has always been closely related to the legend of Merlin and King Arthur."

Molly stood up. "Detective! We are tired. Sick and weary. What does all of this have to do with the murder of our dear child?"

"Everything!" Scotch hissed.

Otter stepped aside and one by one constables began filing into the room and taking up positions along the side walls, back wall and to Scotch's right and left.

Scotch did not look at one of them. Instead, he searched the faces of the Villagers, one by one, the tension building. "It is with great regret that I must announce that you are all under arrest!"

The hall became a storm of angry protests.

Scotch nodded to the nearest constable. Constable Evans. He blew a whistle hanging from his neck and the constables lifted night clubs.

A deathly silence.

Scotch sighed, shook his head, then said. "You have done a great disservice to Merlin's memory and to that of the dear Tennifer and so many other children over these past years."

He shifted uncomfortably, noted that Detective Mallory had risen from her chair and was pale as a ghost.

The Next Morning

"A cult. A blasted cult!" Detective Mallory said, her face contorted with both anger and confusion. "Every one of them all?"

"Yes," Scotch replied. Sadly. "All."

Sherlock Holmes stood next Watson, who was yawning deeply. "Quite well done, Detective."

"Thanks. I do me best."

Otter laughed. "As do Watson and me. On a full stomach."

Detective Mallory sighed. "Well, that is a long way off, isn't it? No one left to cook a meal for us."

Holmes smiled. "I think that problem is solved."

Ms. Hudson exited the Cove Hostelry with two baskets. One in each hand. She smiled.

"I still don't understand how you solved the case as you did," Detective Mallory demanded. "Explain!"

Holmes smiled at her outburst but nodded to Scotch.

Scotch frowned a moment, then said. "I noted that all the villagers had one thing in common."

"Which was?" Detective Mallory asked.

"They all accused each other of the murder."

"But that isn't enough to close a case, is it, Detective McBride," Holmes pointed out with a smile.

Scotch nodded. "No, it was Doctor Watson here, who put the clincher to the case."

Detective Mallory glanced at Watson.

Watson yawned deeply, then said. "The victims all had one thing in common."

"Which was?" Detective Mallory demanded, her frustration growing.

"Broken fingernails."

"They all fought their assailant."

"Assailants," Scotch corrected. "Each of these villagers is guilty of at least one murder in their lifetime."

"Disgusting!" Watson growled.

"Indeed, it is, Watson," Holmes agreed. "But is the death of a child ever agreeable?"

"But surely that didn't point to any evidence the villagers did it," insisted Detective Mallory.

"No, it was not the nail in the coffin. It was when I began noticing one thing in common with all the villagers."

"Which was?"

"They all had scars from scratch marks on their necks, shoulders or arms."

Detective Mallory was silent a moment. "But that still proves nothing."

Holmes clapped a hand on Watson's shoulder. "Which is why dear Watson and I come into the picture. Watson used the Teslascope to examine the tissue beneath the fingernails of all the slain children."

Detective Mallory grunted angrily and faced Scotch again. "Which is why you had me digging up all those graves!"

"Not all. Just enough." He smiled at her. "I want to thank you for your work, without which Watson would have had nothing to examine."

"And you no conclusive evidence," Detective Mallory said with a grudging nod.

"And" Scotch added with a grin that caused Detective Mallory to shrink back. "You got to see that all detective work isn't just fun and games."

Detective Mallory started to complain, then realized she would only be digging her own grave. She had been complaining for weeks now that she did not get to do everything he did.

She crossed her arms over her breasts and bit her tongue.

"Yes. This is what teamwork is all about, is it not, Detective Holmes," Scotch asked.

"Indeed," Holmes replied. "Indeed."

"So, what will happen to this village now?" Watson asked, his voice a tad sad as he surveyed the empty street and buildings.

A Year Later

Scotch, Otter, and Detective Mallory stand at the entrance to the village.

Everything has changed about it.

There are children everywhere and adults playing with them.

"I can't believe it!" Detective Mallory exclaimed, clapping her hands in delight.

"It's the world that children should grow up in," Scotch replied, then hefting a bundle of toys he had brought he entered the village.

Otter hefted his own and followed.

Detective Mallory gave both men a smile they would never see and followed, carrying her own bundle. But not of toys. Something far sweeter. Caramel apples.

The children saw Scotch coming and ran to greet him.

Scotch opened his bag and began passing out toys.

Otter the same.

But Detective Mallory's bag got the most exclamations of joy from the children. "Candy! Candy! Candy!" They all cried.

That night Detective Mallory lay on her bed at the newly renovated Cove. It was now one of many dormitories for the homeless children to sleep and live in. She could not help but think of Scotch McBride and the way he beamed at all the children he passed toys to and played with the entire day and into the night.

She had been wondering for over a year now what kind of man he really was.

As she began to drift off into sleep, she knew the answer. And it was one that touched her heart.

Deeply.